For Flea

First U.S. edition 2007

Library of Congress Cataloging-in-Publication Data is available.

Library of Congress Catalog Card Number 2006049077

ISBN 978-0-7636-3381-3

2 4 6 8 10 9 7 5 3 1

Printed in China

This book was typeset in ITC Usherwood Medium.
The illustrations were done in pencil and watercolor.

Candlewick Press
2067 Massachusetts Avenue
Cambridge, Massachusetts 02140

visit us at www.candlewick.com

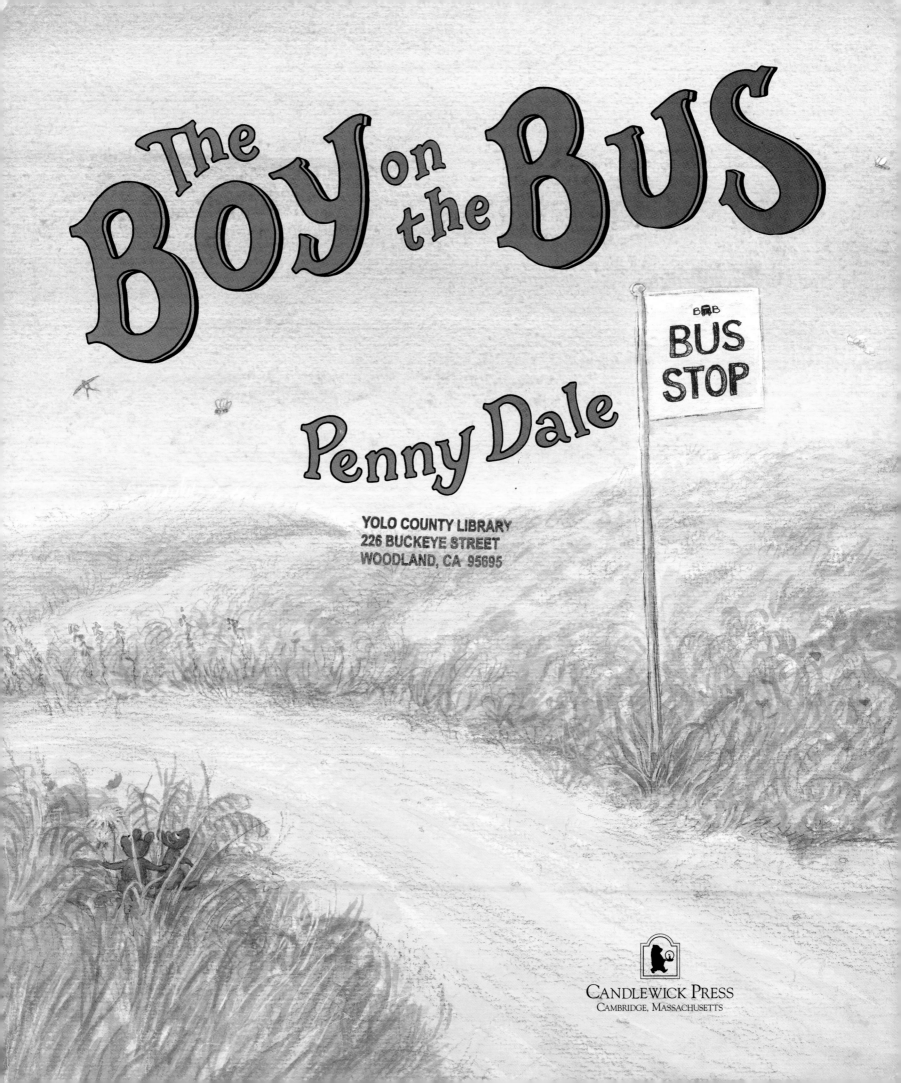

The BOY on the BUS

Penny Dale

BUS STOP

CANDLEWICK PRESS
CAMBRIDGE, MASSACHUSETTS

The boy on the bus drives
round and round,
round and round,
round and round.
The boy on the bus drives
round and round.

Who wants to ride on the bus?

Ducks!

The boy on the bus says, "Up you come!
Tickets here! Lots of room!"

The boy on the bus says, "All aboard!
Ready, steady, go!"

The ducks on the bus go
Quack quack quack!
Quack quack quack!
Quack quack quack!
The ducks on the bus go
Quack quack quack!

Who wants to ride on the bus?

Pigs!

The boy on the bus says, "On you get!
Take a seat! Not full yet!"

The boy on the bus says, "All aboard!
Ready, steady, go!"

The pigs on the bus go
Oink oink oink!
Oink oink oink!
Oink oink oink!
The pigs on the bus go
Oink oink oink!

Who wants to

ride on the bus?

Cows! A horse!

Chickens!   Goats!

The boy on the bus says, "Room inside!

Move on back! Enjoy the ride!"

The boy on the bus says, "All aboard!
Ready, steady, go!"

The cows on the bus go
Moo moo moo!
The horse on the bus goes
Neigh neigh neigh!
The chickens on the bus go
Cluck cluck cluck!
The goats on the bus go
Bleat bleat bleat!

Who wants to ride on the bus?

Sheep!

The boy on the bus says, "What a crowd!

Climb up here! Careful now!"

The boy on the bus says, "Hold on tight!
Ready, steady, go!"

The sheep on the bus go
Baa baa baa!
Baa baa baa!
Baa baa baa!
The sheep on the bus go
Baa baa baa!

BUS

BOY 1

READY, STEADY, GO!

The wheels on the bus go
round and round,
round and round,
round and round.
The wheels on the bus go
round and round

Baa baa!

Baa!

Baa!

Baa baa!

Baa baa!

Baaaaaa!

Baaaaaa!

Baaaa baa!

Quack!
Quack!

Baa baa!

Mooooo!

Moooo!

Cluck cluck!

Bleat!
Bleat!

Bleeeat!

Oink oink!

Oink oink!

Quack!
Quack!

Neigh!
Neigh!

all day long!